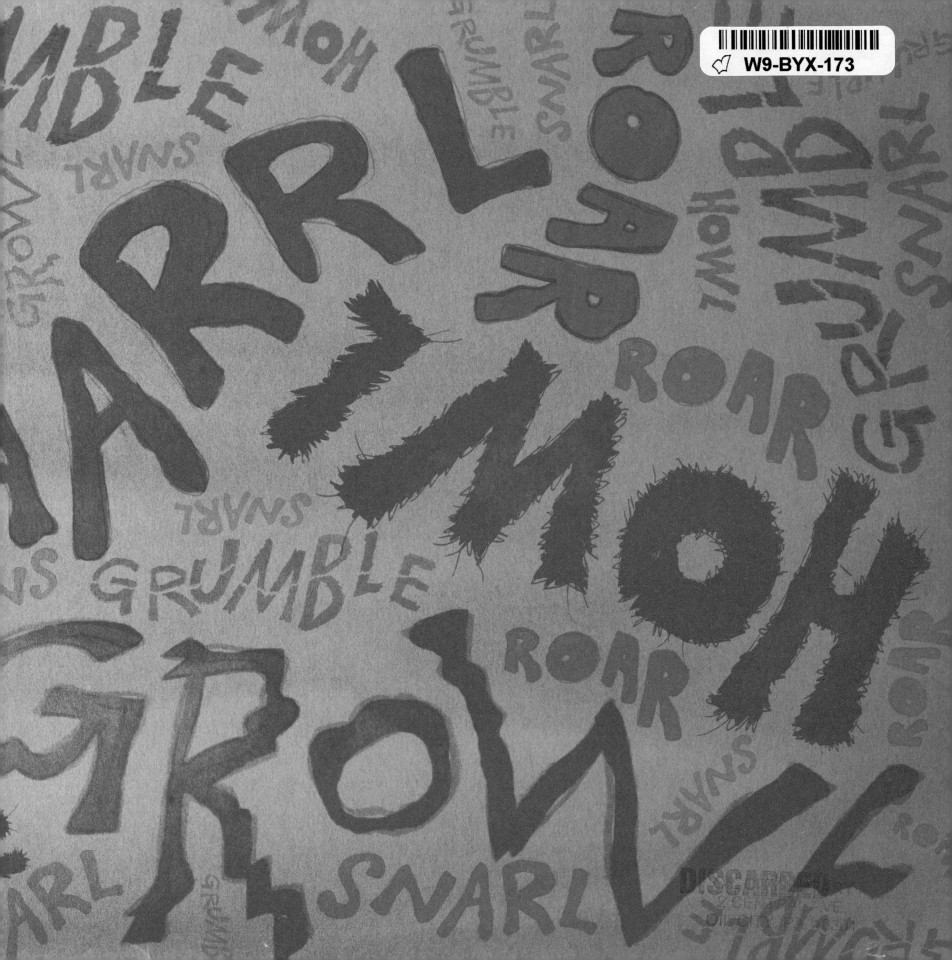

EVEN MONSTERS...

by AJ Smith

Thank you to my wife, Karen. This whole book thing isn't possible without your support
(and continued tolerance of my unbreakable drawing habit).

The illustrations in this book were cooked up using only the finest USDA organic ingredients: pencil scribbles, acrylic splatters, cut paper, computer magic, and genuine, honest-to-goodness Crayolas!

Published by Sourcebooks Jabberwocky, an imprint of Sourcebooks, Inc.

P.O. Box 4410, Naperville, Illinois 60567-4410

(630) 961-3900

Fax: (630) 961-2168

www.jabberwockykids.com

Library of Congress Cataloging-in-Publication data is on file with the publisher.

Source of Production: Leo Paper, Heshan City, Guangdong Province, China

Date of Production: January 2014

Run Number: 22048

Printed and bound in China .

LEO 10 9 8 7 6 5 4 3 2 1

sourcebooks
jabberwocky

Even roaring monsters put on
clean underwear in the morning.

They eat a well-rounded breakfast

and comb the cooties out of their fur.

Everybody knows monsters SNARL!

But did you know...

Even snarling monsters ride the bus to school.

They learn their ABC's

and draw in art class.

Everybody knows monsters GRUMBLE!

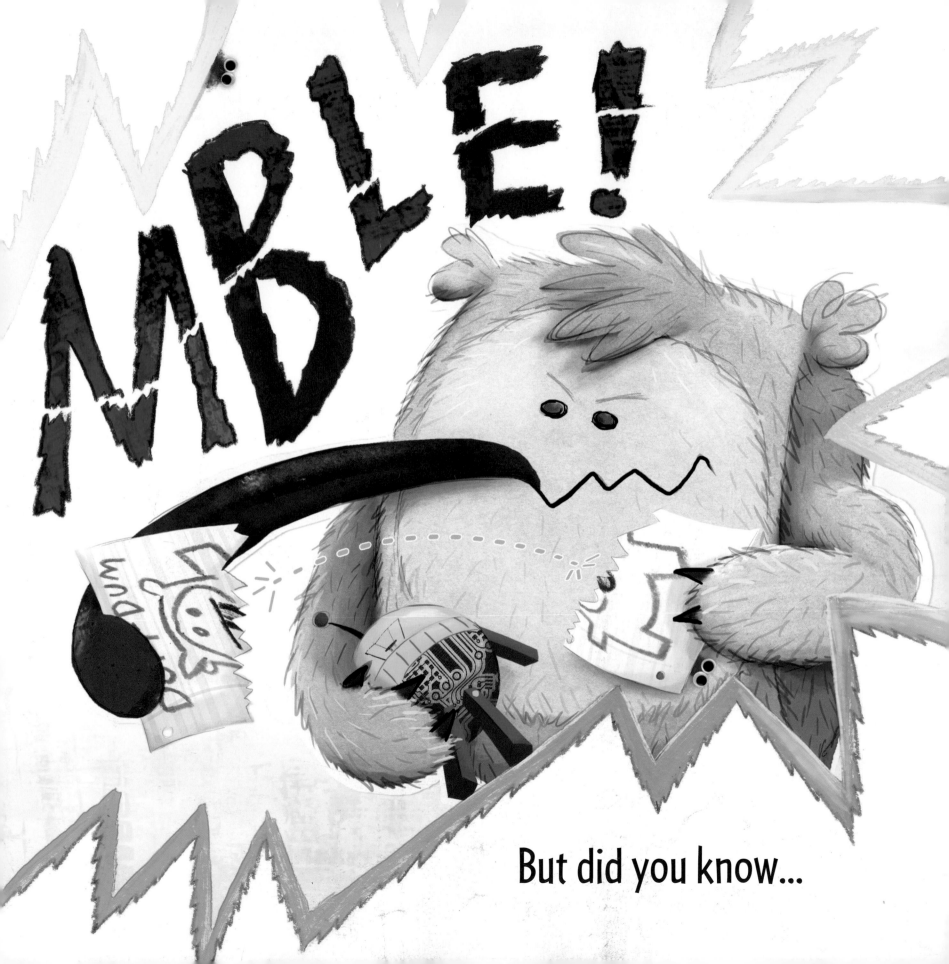

But did you know...

Even grumbling monsters love soccer.

They hide in tree forts

Everybody knows monsters GROWL!

But did you know...

Even growling monsters
have to finish their dinner,

take a bath,
and brush their teeth.

But did you know...

Sometimes even the most roaring, snarling, grumbling, growling, howling monsters are afraid of the dark.

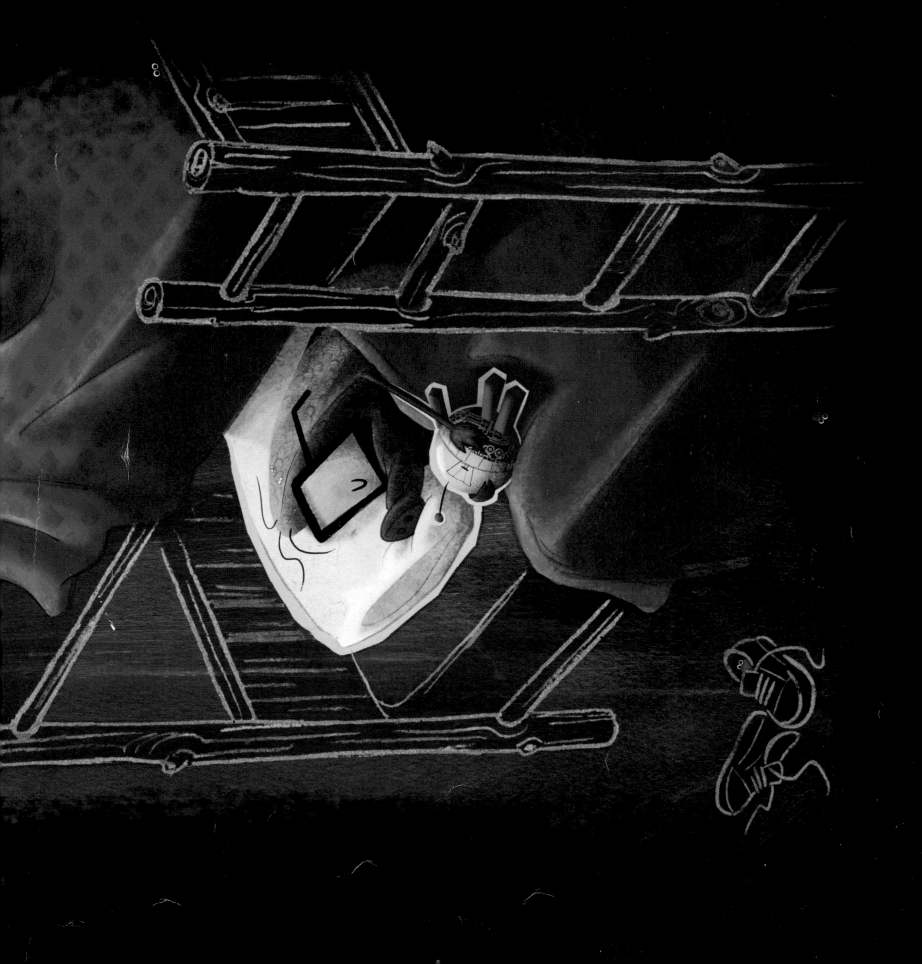

Sometimes even monsters

need a kiss goodnight.

There's more to the story...

EVEN MONSTERS.com

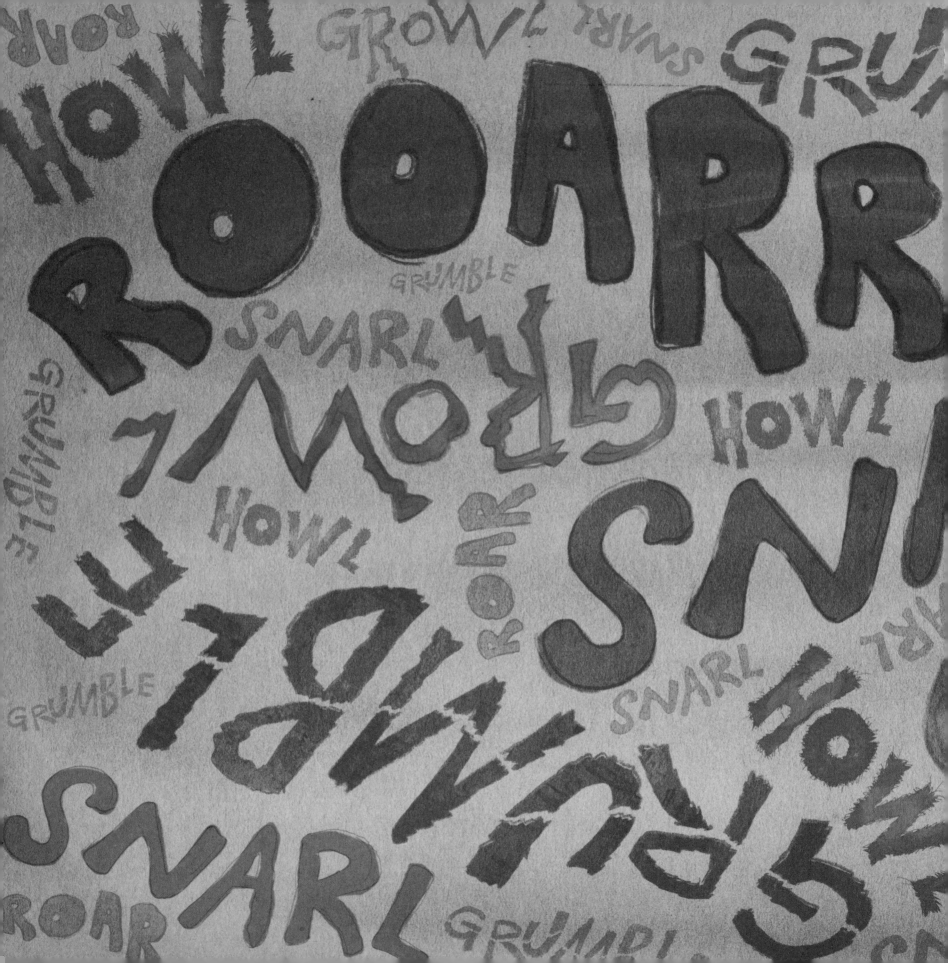